The Gingerbread Man in Winter

Elizabeth Walker

Illustrated by John Richardson

Beaver Books

Also in Beaver by Elizabeth Walker

The Adventures of the Gingerbread Man

Contents

A Beaver Book
Published by Arrow Books Limited
62-65 Chandos Place, London WC2N 4NW

An imprint of Century Hutchinson Limited

London Melbourne Sydney Auckland
Johannesburg and agencies throughout
the world

First pubilshed by Hutchinson Children's Books 1987
Beaver edition 1988

Set in Baskerville
by BookEns, Saffron Walden, Essex

Printed and bound in Great Britain by
Anchor Brendon Limited, Tiptree, Essex

ISBN 0 09 955420 8

The Gingerbread Man's Winter Poem

I'm the gingerbread man, do you know about me?
I'm clever and handsome and brave as can be.
I run and I jump and I race all about,
And when I am happy I sing and I shout!

I was baked in an oven, placed in a pan,
And no one could catch me when from it I ran.
The fox and the crow chase me all through
    the day,
But Gingerbread dashes and races away!

I have lots of friends and I have lots of fun,
I have told you about my days in the sun.
But winter has come with its ice and its snow –
Now what will happen? Well, who can know?

1

The Gingerbread Man
and the Snow

It was winter. Every day the gingerbread man peeped out of his haystack, where he lived all warm and snug, and wondered if the sun would be shining. Sometimes it was, but mostly the sky was grey, the wind was blowing and it was cold. But that didn't stop the gingerbread man running and jumping through the fields and the meadows, singing his song.

'The wind is so cold and the sky is so grey,
But the gingerbread man will still come out and play.
For I have a coat that's all cosy and warm,
So I don't care a bit for the horridest storm!'

And he skipped and hopped among the frosty tussocks of grass.

But when he woke up one morning and looked out of his haystack he was most surprised: there wasn't any grass; there weren't any hedges; and even the trees looked strange, all covered in fluffy white. The gingerbread man stared and stared, then he reached out his gingerbread hand to see what it was that was covering everything. 'Ooh!' he said to himself. 'This is very, very cold, even colder than the frost.' And he tasted some of it, just to see if it was good to eat. But it didn't taste of anything except cold.

The gingerbread man put on his conker hat and the coat and socks Mrs Rabbit had made for him, and set out to find someone to tell him what had happened. Flump! As soon as the gingerbread man stepped out of his haystack he fell right down into the soft, fluffy white.

'This is very strange,' he said to himself. 'I can't run and jump at all.' But he kept on trying, flump, flump, flump! 'Stop it!' cried the gingerbread man crossly. 'Go away you horrid stuff. I'm the gingerbread man and you must let me run and jump and play.'

'Caark! Caark!' came a harsh voice. It was the crow, huddled in a bare tree, his dirty feathers all on end. 'Haven't seen snow before, have you Gingerbread Man? Nasty cold stuff it is – no use talking to snow.'

'Why is it here?' asked the gingerbread man, his conker hat over one eye. 'It won't let me run and jump, and I don't like it!' He struggled to his feet and tried to give a very little skip. Flump! Down he fell again and the snow went up his nose and made him sneeze.

'Well, well, well,' said the crow, moving along his branch. 'Seems to me a gingerbread man what can't run and jump would make a tasty bite for a poor old crow. A body needs something to keep him warm in winter.' And he flapped his dirty wings and flew into the air, right towards the little gingerbread man

'Oh! Oh! Oh!' cried the gingerbread man, and he tried to run away. But the snow wouldn't let him! Flump, flump, flump he went; and then a great big flump right into the middle of a deep snowdrift. The gingerbread man kept his eyes tightly shut, expecting at any moment to be seized by the crow's sharp claws. But nothing happened! He opened his eyes slowly, to find that he was completely covered with snow. He couldn't see the crow anywhere, but he could hear him, muttering and flapping his wings.

'Where's that little gingerbread man? Where's he gone? Just when I wanted a tasty bite of gingerbread.' And he flew away, back to his nest.

The little gingerbread man struggled to his feet. Out popped his head into the daylight. 'Thank you for hiding me, snow,' he said. 'Perhaps I might like you after all.' And on he struggled, flump, flump, flump!

Suddenly there was a great rushing sound. 'Look out!' cried a voice, but before the gingerbread man could move something whizzed past him, down the slope and into the snowy hedge. It was the otter, laughing all over his brown, whiskery face.

'Hello Gingerbread Man,' he said happily. 'Isn't snow fun!'

'No,' said the gingerbread man, who was tired of flumping. 'Will it always be here now?'

The otter thumped his wide tail and made snow showers. 'Dear me no! Here today, gone tomorrow, that's snow. Or sometimes the day after. What's the matter – got your warm clothes on haven't you?'

'Yes,' said the gingerbread man. 'But I can't run and jump. Every time I try I just go flump!'

The otter leaned back and laughed. 'Who wants to run and jump when they can slide?' he chuckled. 'Come on Gingerbread, I'll show you how!'

So together they went flump, flump, flump! to the top of the slope. The otter dug down in the snow and found a big brown leaf for the gingerbread man to sit on. 'Now,' he said. 'Hold on tight. Off you go!' And he gave the little gingerbread man a great big push.

Wheee! Off flew the gingerbread man's conker hat. He went so fast down the slope his currant eyes began to smart. Flump! He landed in the

deep snow by the hedge and a minute later the otter slid down on his tail to join him.

'What do you think of that young feller?' said the otter, laughing.

The gingerbread man just clapped his gingerbread hands and laughed too.

All day they played in the snow, sliding and sliding. At last, as it was getting dark, the gingerbread man grew tired. 'I must go back to my haystack,' he said to his friend. 'Will the snow be here tomorrow?'

'Maybe it will, maybe it won't,' said the otter, picking up the gingerbread man's conker hat and plonking it on his head. 'Make sure you brush down now young feller. Don't want you getting damp. Snow melts, you know.'

The little gingerbread man yawned. 'Thank you, Otter, for sliding with me. I think I do like snow after all.' And he began to flump, flump, flump! his way home.

2

The Gingerbread Man
Saves the Day

The next day when the gingerbread man looked out of his haystack he was very surprised to see that the snow had almost gone. Some of it was still there, in piles by the hedges, but it wasn't white and pretty any more, just dirty and wet. 'How strange you are, snow,' said the little gingerbread man. 'I wonder where you have gone to?' He didn't know that the snow had turned to water, just as it always does.

The gingerbread man decided to go out for a walk. But no sooner had he left the haystack than the wind blew his conker hat right off! 'Winter is very strange,' said the gingerbread man to himself, chasing after it. 'Rain and snow and wind! I must be careful or I shall be blown into crumbs.' And he kept close to the shelter of the hedge, holding tight to his hat and keeping his coat fastened.

The wind moaned, hoooo, hoooo! and blew old leaves and yellow grass into the air. It was so noisy that at first the gingerbread man didn't hear anything else. Then he put his head on one side. He could hear faint voices. 'Help! Squeak! Help!'

'Someone is in trouble,' said the gingerbread man, and he began to run and jump as quickly as he could, and as he ran he sang a song.

'The wind is so fierce and blowing so strong,
But a gingerbread man can tell something's wrong!
I'll run and I'll dash till I see what's to do,
For someone's in trouble and soon I'll know who!'

The cries were coming from the edge of the field, where the grass was taller than the gingerbread man. 'Caark! Caark!' he heard, and the squeaking was louder still.

'Someone's being chased by that crow,' he said to himself, and dashed bravely into the grass.

The grass stems were as thick as a forest and the gingerbread man struggled to get through. Suddenly he saw what was wrong. The little round nest of grass that was the home of the harvest mice lay blown to the ground, and around it ran all the little mice squeaking, 'Squeak, squeak, squeak, squeak, squeak.'

'Caark! Caark!' called the crow, flapping in the hedge. 'I shall eat a tasty little mouse, I shall!'

'Oh no you won't,' said the gingerbread man, and at once he began to catch hold of the little

mice as they ran about, gathering them safely together. But they wouldn't stay still! As soon as he caught one and looked for another, the first little mouse ran away, round and round the nest. Again and again the gingerbread man caught them, but as soon as he let them go they ran off calling, 'Ma! Pa!' and squeaking.

At last the gingerbread man stopped and put his hands on his hips. He was out of breath and he knew that if he didn't gather up the baby mice soon the crow would eat them. 'Mr Mouse! Mr Mouse! Where are you?' he called. But all he could hear was the wind, and the little mice squeaking, and the crow calling, 'Caark! Caark!'

from the hedge. 'Mr Mouse! Mr Mouse! Where are you?' he called again.

Just then he heard a very strange sound. Cor – phew it went, and again cor – phew. It was coming from the mice's nest, which lay broken on the floor. The little gingerbread man went across and looked inside. There, curled up tight, were Mr and Mrs Mouse, fast asleep. 'Wake up!' cried the gingerbread man very loudly. 'Your children are in danger!'

At once the two mice opened their eyes and looked sleepily about. 'What's happening? What is it? Is it spring?' they said, rubbing their eyes.

'Where are those naughty children?' said Mrs Mouse, and clapped her paws together calling, 'Mice! Mice! Where are you?'

And all the little mice, hearing their mother's voice, stopped running about and squeaking and rushed to the nest, all talking at once. 'Ma, we crashed! Ma, I'm hungry! Ma, what are we going to do now our house is all broken?'

'Why, so it is,' said Mr Mouse, looking at the nest. 'We must build a new one. Come wife, come children, let's set to work.'

Just then the crow gave a loud, 'Caark!' from the hedge. All the mice clung to each other.

'We shall be eaten!' said Mr Mouse fearfully. And the little mice went, 'Squeak, squeak, squeak, squeak, squeak!'

'Don't worry,' said the gingerbread man bravely. 'There's nothing a crow likes as much as a gingerbread man.' And off he ran, out of the tall grass and away across the field, skipping and jumping.

As soon as the crow saw him he flapped into the air, saying, 'Gingerbread! Gingerbread! That's what a body needs on a windy day.'

'You can't catch me,' cried the gingerbread man, and he sang a little song.

'The wind blew the mice from their nest to
   the ground,

And the crow thought it was a *fine* feast that
  he'd found!
But Gingerbread saved them as brave as can be.
That silly old crow, he won't ever catch me!'

And with an extra big jump he landed safe in his
haystack. Snap went the crow's sharp beak, right
outside. 'I'm not scared at all,' said the gingerbread man, putting his nose in the air. 'That silly
crow won't ever catch me!'

Outside the crow rattled his feathers and
snapped his beak again. 'Won't I indeed?' he
croaked. 'Just you wait and see little gingerbread man!'

3

The Gingerbread Man
Gets Caught

The gingerbread man woke up and at once stuck his head out of the haystack to see what sort of day it was. The sun was shining, and though it was cold, a robin was hopping about on the ground pecking at seeds.

'Hello,' said the gingerbread man cheerfully, pulling on his coat. 'This is a fine day. I think the sun's pleased with me for saving the harvest mice yesterday.' And he swung his conker hat from one hand and did a little dance.

'Think a lot of yourself, don't you?' said the robin, putting his head on one side and watching the gingerbread man out of his beady black eye.

'I do think I'm very brave,' said the gingerbread man. 'And I am made out of the finest gingerbread. I have daisy buttons too.'

'Well I'm pretty smart if it comes to that,' said the robin. 'Look at my fine red breast. I'm a handsome bird, I am.'

'You are quite handsome,' said the gingerbread man. 'But not as handsome as me.' And he ran away across the field, singing his song.

'I'm the gingerbread man on a winter's day,
Looking for lots of new games to play.
Not even the robin's as handsome as me,
And I'm braver than anyone else could be!'

The gingerbread man was so busy singing he ran right across the middle of the field without any thought of danger. Swish! Out of the sky swept a great black shadow. It was the crow, stretching sharp claws to snatch up the little gingerbread man. 'Oh! Oh! Oh!' cried the gingerbread man, racing this way and that. 'Go away, Crow! Go away!' But the crow flapped his great wings and clattered his dirty feathers, as close as anything.

'Who's so clever now!' he croaked, snapping his hard beak.

'Help!' cried the little gingerbread man, running as fast as he could. 'Help!'

It was no use. The gingerbread man was too far from the edge of the field and he could not run to safety. The crow reached out his yellow claws and snatched the gingerbread man up from the ground. 'Now I have you Gingerbread Man,' shouted the crow. 'Now we shall see how brave you are!' And he flapped his dirty black wings and began to fly back to his nest.

At first the gingerbread man struggled, but he was so far from the ground he was afraid he might fall. So he stopped struggling and said to himself, 'I see I have been foolish. I don't feel very brave at all and if the crow eats me up I won't even be handsome. Oh dear! Whatever shall I do?'

'Caark! Caark!' called the crow. 'Look at this, Mrs Crow. I've brought you a tasty bit of gingerbread!' And he landed with a swoosh on his messy, twiggy nest.

The gingerbread man got to his feet, pulling his coat into place. He felt very frightened, but he did not show it. 'He's a very small bit of gingerbread,' said Mrs Crow, who was just as dirty as her husband and had a beak that crossed over at the end. 'I thought you said you was going to bring me a decent meal!'

The crow looked a little upset. 'I'm sorry dear,' he said humbly. 'It's very hard catching a gingerbread man.'

'Hard! Hard! You telling me it's hard to catch something as small as that?' Mrs Crow stared at the gingerbread man so fiercely he shook. But still he didn't show it.

'Excuse me,' he said rather shyly. 'I really am quite hard to catch.'

Mrs Crow gave a horrible cackle. '*He* might find you hard to catch, I'll grant you that. Wouldn't take *me* five minutes.'

The gingerbread man smiled. 'What you laughing at?' demanded Mrs Crow. 'If I didn't have this nest to look after I'd catch a gingerbread man every day! Wouldn't I Crow?'

'Yes dear,' said the crow humbly. But again the gingerbread man smiled.

'I would! I would!' shouted Mrs Crow, bouncing up and down so hard that bits of twig fell from the nest to the ground. 'Put him down, Crow, and watch me catch him!'

The crow looked so upset that for a moment the gingerbread man thought that all was lost. But then, sighing, the crow took hold of the

gingerbread man once again and carried him down to the ground.

'I'll give you a start,' called Mrs Crow, high in the tree. 'I'll count to five.'

'All right,' called the gingerbread man.

Now the crows had made their nest in a tree at the edge of a big, dark wood. As soon as Mrs Crow began counting, 'One – two – three – four – five,' the gingerbread man ran as fast as ever he could towards the trees.

'Coming!' called Mrs Crow, flapping her dusty wings. The gingerbread man ran faster still, and as he ran he sang this song.

'The gingerbread man is running away,
He won't be a meal for a crow today.
He'll run and he'll dash right into this wood,
To find some adventures, like Gingerbread
    should!'

Away he ran, into the trees where Mrs Crow
could not catch him. She spun round in the air
and shouted crossly, 'Crow! Crow! He tricked
me, Crow! I want some gingerbread!' And the
crow, sitting on the nest, said miserably, 'Blast
that little gingerbread man!'

4

The Gingerbread Man
and the Badger

It was still quite early in the day when the ginger-bread man found himself in the wood. 'I don't suppose Red Fox is out and about yet,' he said in a small voice. He didn't dare go out of the wood in case the crows caught him, but he wasn't sure he wanted to stay in the wood in case Red Fox liked the look of him for her dinner! 'Perhaps I'm not so brave after all,' he said sadly. 'And I wasn't very clever to let that crow catch me.' Sighing, he plodded off down a path.

Suddenly, there was a loud rustling in the undergrowth, and then a rumbling, and a grunting. 'Oh dear me,' said the gingerbread man, stopping. His gingerbread knees shook with fright. 'I do hope it isn't Red Fox,' he said to himself.

The rumbling and grunting came closer, and then closer still. 'It's a very large and noisy thing,' said the gingerbread man. 'If I wasn't a ginger-bread man I should be very frightened indeed.' And his knees shook still more.

CRASH! The thing burst on to the path in

front of him. 'Oh! Oh! Oh!' cried the ginger-bread man, turning to run away.

'Ho there young fella!' called a deep voice. 'Where are you running to?'

The gingerbread man stopped. He felt a little foolish. 'Hello Badger,' he said shyly. 'I wasn't running anywhere really.'

'You seem in a hurry for someone going nowhere,' said the badger, who was a little cross because it was past his bedtime. 'And your coat has holes. What's been happening? Come on, out with it!'

The gingerbread man put his hands behind his back. 'The crow caught me,' he said sadly. 'But I escaped and ran into the wood. I thought you might be Red Fox.'

The badger stroked his bristly whiskers. 'Well, I might have been. This wood's no place for a little gingerbread man. Better stay with me till Crow's forgotten about you. Yes, that's the best thing. Come along now, come along!' And off he crashed through the undergrowth, with the gingerbread man hopping and skipping behind.

Soon they came to a hole in a large bank of earth. 'Here we are,' said Badger. 'Follow me, now.' And into the hole he went, snuffling and grunting all the time.

It was very dark in the badger sett, and the ground was covered with dried leaves. 'Nothing

like leaves to make a soft bed,' said Badger, settling himself down to sleep. 'Turn in, young fella, and be quick about it.'

'I'm not sleepy,' said the gingerbread man.

'That's as may be,' said Badger. 'But I went a long way last night and I'm ready for a bit of shut-eye. No noise now! I'll see you safe out of the wood this evening.' And snuggling down in the leaves, the badger fell fast asleep.

The gingerbread man wondered what to do. First he made patterns with the leaves, flower patterns and tree patterns, and then patterns that weren't anything at all. After that he began to explore the sett, but when his boots made a noise in the leaves the badger grunted and grumbled as if he was about to wake up, and the gingerbread man had to stand quite still until he settled down again. He thought perhaps he might be tired after all, so he lay down and tried to go to sleep. He turned this way and that, and that way and this, and he scratched his nose and his arm and his tummy, but still he couldn't go to sleep. So he sat up and sang a little song to himself, very quietly.

'The gingerbread man went into the trees,
And met a kind badger, whose home's full of
    leaves.
He's sleeping and snoring all through the day,
And that isn't at all the Gingerbread way!'

At long last the badger began to wake up, stretching and snuffling to himself and shaking his great black-and-white body. Then he caught sight of the gingerbread man. 'Goodness me! What are you doing here young fella?'

'You promised to take me out of the wood,' said the gingerbread man politely.

'Did I? Why so I did. What are we waiting for then, come along, come along!' And off bustled the badger, with the gingerbread man close behind.

Outside it was evening, and very cold. The gingerbread man stayed close to the badger, looking this way and that into the dark shadows.

Red Fox would like a piece of gingerbread on a cold evening. The owls were hooting in the far trees, hoooo, hoooo, hoooo! He shivered and pulled his warm coat close about him, following the badger along the twisting paths. At the edge of the wood the badger stopped.

'This is your way young fella. Daresay you'll want to be out and about now it's dark. Fine cold night for a stroll.'

'I usually go to bed at night,' said the gingerbread man shyly.

The badger looked surprised. 'Do you? Dashed strange habits you young people have nowadays. On your way then, and take a bit more care in future!'

'I will,' promised the gingerbread man, and began to skip across the field in the moonlight.

Suddenly he stopped. 'I'm not at all tired,' he said to himself. 'And I've a fine coat to keep me warm. The crow is fast asleep and the fox is in the wood, so I shall run and jump and have a nighttime adventure!'

And that is just what the gingerbread man did.

5

The Gingerbread Man and the Night-time Adventure

The moon was shining with a clear, cold light when the gingerbread man set out on his adventure. 'How pretty everything is,' he said to himself. 'The crow is in his nest and Red Fox is in the wood, so I really have nothing to be afraid of at all.' And he went running and jumping over the silvery grass. He sang a night-time song.

'The gingerbread man's going out in the night,
And the world lit by moonlight's a wonderful
    sight.
The shadows are dark and the wind is so cold,
But a man made of gingerbread has to be
    bold!'

And after that he wasn't even the smallest bit frightened of the night.

Just then he heard a rather strange sound. 'Boo,' it went. 'Boo, hoo, hoo!' And then, 'Boo, hoo, hoo,' again.

'What a dreadful noise,' said the gingerbread man. 'I must find out what is making it.' So he ran quickly across the grass to the hedge.

There, sitting on the frosty ground, was a very small, very sad little fox. When it saw the gingerbread man it opened its wide mouth and said, 'Boo, hoo, hoo!' so loudly that the gingerbread man put his hands to his gingerbread head.

'What a terrible noise,' he said crossly. 'Why are you doing it, little fox?'

'I've lost my mummy,' wailed the fox cub, and said, 'Boo, hoo, hoo,' once more.

'Do you mean Red Fox?' asked the gingerbread man.

The fox cub wiped his eyes with the end of his fine bushy tail. 'Yes,' he sniffed. 'She told me to stay on the path, but I saw a mouse and I chased it. And now I shall never get back to the den, and I shan't have any dinner and I shan't see my mummy!'

The gingerbread man knew that it was up to him to see the little fox safely home. 'If you'll stop that noise I'll take you to Red Fox,' he said, although even thinking of it made him shake with fright.

But at once the fox cub cheered up. 'Will you really?' he said. 'Oh please take me home. I'll always do what my mummy tells me, I'll never be naughty again.' And because he was so pleased he put out his long tongue and licked the gingerbread man's face. 'Ooh!' he said, his eyes big and round. 'You taste nicer than anything.'

The gingerbread man stepped back quickly. 'I don't think you should eat people who are trying to help you,' he said.

'I won't,' said the fox cub, looking a little ashamed. 'But you do taste very nice.'

'So I should,' said the gingerbread man. 'I *am* made out of gingerbread, after all.'

They set off, the gingerbread man running along in front and the fox cub following close behind. Soon they saw the wood in front of them, dark and dangerous.

'This is where you live,' said the gingerbread man, stopping. 'Off you go.'

The fox cub looked about him, a worried expression on his furry face. 'I think it is our wood, but where's our den? And where's my mummy?' And he began to wail again, 'Boo, hoo, hoo!' just as loud as before.

'But I can't take you any further,' said the gingerbread man, tipping his conker hat back on his head. 'Red Fox will eat me!'

The little fox stopped crying and sat down. 'Well – she might,' he said. 'My mummy has strong white teeth that go snap, snap, snap. But she might not eat you. After all you did find me when I was lost.'

The gingerbread man looked rather worriedly about him. But the fox cub had to get home and there wasn't anyone else who could take him. So

the little gingerbread man marched bravely into the deep, dark wood.

Away in the far trees the owls hunted, their quiet wings gliding through the air. Close at hand creatures rustled in the bare bushes, out on their night-time business. But the gingerbread man hurried along, and after him padded the little fox cub.

Suddenly Red Fox stepped from the shadows, her coat gleaming in the moonlight, her tail thick and glossy. 'Mummy!' cried the fox cub and ran to her.

Red Fox put an elegant paw round him. 'I have searched for you everywhere,' she said.

'My friend found me,' said the fox cub. 'And Mummy, he tastes so good!'

The little gingerbread man took a step backwards. Red Fox and her cub licked their red lips and their sharp teeth gleamed. 'Dear child,' said the fox, sighing, 'we cannot eat people who help us. Why don't you come to our den and meet my other children, Gingerbread Man?'

'No thank you,' said the gingerbread man politely. 'I really must be getting home.'

'I didn't really think my mummy would eat you,' said the fox cub. 'Thank you for helping me, Gingerbread Man.'

The gingerbread man didn't say anything. He turned and ran as fast as he could to the edge of the wood and out into the moonlit fields. Then he began skipping and jumping back to his hay-stack, singing his song.

'The wood in the dark is so wild and so black,
It isn't for Gingerbread, he's running back!
When Owl and Badger and Fox start to creep,
Then a gingerbread man is better asleep!'

The haystack seemed warm and safe and comfortable as the gingerbread man took off his hat and coat and boots. 'This is better than a badger's sett, and it's nicer than night-time adventures,' he said to himself. And in no time at all the gingerbread man was fast asleep.

6

The Gingerbread Man
at Christmas

One morning when the gingerbread man was out running and jumping, he noticed that everyone seemed very busy. As he passed the rabbit burrow all the little rabbits were outside, tying up little bunches of holly with pieces of grass, and then helping to wrap four late blackberries in a leaf.

'Why are you doing that?' asked the gingerbread man. 'What is it for?'

'It's for our mum,' said a little rabbit shyly. 'For Christmas.'

Now the gingerbread man didn't know about Christmas, but didn't like to say so. Instead he said, 'Oh yes. Christmas!' and went on his way, pulling his coat around him. It wasn't as warm a coat as it had been, because the crow had made holes in it and sometimes the gingerbread man had caught it on hedges and thistles when he was running and jumping. The wind that day was cold, ruffling the feathers of the crow as he pecked at the hard ground. The gingerbread man shrank back when he saw him, but the crow called out, 'Haven't time to catch you today, Gingerbread! A crow's got to look to his Christmas dinner a crow has!' And he pecked harder, gathering seeds and grubs to take back to his nest. Of course the gingerbread man still didn't know what he meant. But he nodded and said, 'Oh yes. Christmas!' once again, just as if he did.

The gingerbread man went on his way. Soon he came to the tall brown winter grass where the harvest mice lived. Mr and Mrs Mouse were rushing to and fro and all the mouse babies were running after them, crying, 'Is it now Ma? Is it tonight Pa? What will I get?' Mr and Mrs Mouse hardly noticed the gingerbread man, as they rushed this way and that saying to one another, 'How will we ever be done before Christmas? Hurry dear, hurry!'

The gingerbread man felt a little sad that no one wanted to talk to him. He walked on, hardly skipping and jumping at all, his hands tucked under his arms to keep warm and his coat blowing in the cold wind. Suddenly Red Fox scampered past. 'Out of my way Gingerbread Man,' she said shortly. 'No time to waste at Christmas. My children are waiting.' The gingerbread man could bear it no longer. 'Red Fox – what is Christmas?' he called.

The fox stopped and turned round, her red

tail swishing. 'Goodness me,' she said to herself. 'He doesn't even know about Christmas.'

'Is it nice?' asked the gingerbread man, stepping a little nearer.

'I should say it is,' said the fox, snapping her white teeth. 'It's about the nicest thing there is. Be off with you Gingerbread Man, I have work to do.' And away she went, her red legs racing.

The gingerbread man felt very sad that he hadn't got a Christmas. He sang a little song to himself as he went slowly back to his haystack.

'Christmas is coming, I know that is true,
But what is Gingerbread meant to do?
All the rabbits and foxes and crows rush
    along,
And a gingerbread man sings a very sad song.'

Just then he passed Mrs Rabbit's burrow. She was standing outside, shaking a duster. 'Well then little gingerbread man,' she said. 'You look very glum. Don't you know it's Christmas?'

'I do know,' said the gingerbread man sadly. 'But I haven't got one.'

Mrs Rabbit held her plump sides and gurgled with laughter. 'Of course you've got Christmas, everybody has. Listen!'

Far away across the frosty fields came the sound of bells, ding dong, ding dong, and then dong, dong, dong! And there was singing, so high and clear that the gingerbread man put his hands to his face and said, 'Oh!' very softly.

'There you are,' said Mrs Rabbit. 'And just you remember to put your sock by your bed tonight. Tomorrow we shall have *such* a dinner, so you run and jump on your way here and make sure you're hungry!'

'Oh thank you Mrs Rabbit,' said the little gingerbread man, skipping with joy. 'But why must I put my sock by my bed?'

'Just you wait and see,' said Mrs Rabbit. 'Be off with you, I'm rushed off my feet today.'

The little gingerbread man went on his way much more happily. And that night, when he settled down in the hay to sleep, he put his sock close by, just to see what would happen. But he couldn't go to sleep! In the fields all around the little animals were whispering and giggling to each other, and sometimes, faintly, there was the sound of bells. The gingerbread man peeped out of his haystack. The stars were like frost across the sky, and one big star shone so brightly the gingerbread man thought it was the most beautiful star he had ever seen.

Then he heard something! A faint jingling sound and a deep voice crying, 'On, on, my beauties. We must be done before morning.'

'What can it be?' said the gingerbread man to himself. The jingling was louder now and there

was the sound of hooves racing through the night. Closer and closer it came, and the little gingerbread man knelt to look out of his haystack and felt very small and very afraid! 'I think this is Christmas,' he whispered to himself. 'What a strange and wonderful thing it is.'

Suddenly a great voice boomed out, 'Whoa my beauties! This little man's still awake – a gingerbread man too, well, well, well. Now, where is my stardust?' And all at once the gingerbread man's currant eyes were filled with glittering stars falling down out of the sky. The next thing he knew it was morning!

'Somebody has filled my sock up,' he said crossly. 'I can't put it on.' And he picked up his sock, as round and fat as anything, and reached inside to see what was there. First he pulled out a red and green scarf! Then he found some walnuts, big and tasty. Last of all he found a brand new coat and boots. 'Oh, thank you, thank you Christmas!' said the gingerbread man, bouncing up and down with joy.

He put on his new scarf, his new coat and his shiny new boots, and filled his pockets with walnuts. Then he set off for Mrs Rabbit's house. He passed the harvest mice, each little mouse child with a brand new hat. 'Happy Christmas, Happy Christmas, Happy Christmas, Happy Christmas, Happy Christmas,' they called.

Mr Mouse said, 'Compliments of the Season.'

Even the crow flapped out of his bare tree and called, 'Caark! Caark! Happy Christmas Gingerbread Man!'

When he reached Mrs Rabbit's house he felt a little shy as all the rabbits rushed out to meet him. 'I've brought these,' he said, taking out his walnuts.

'Well! That is kind,' said Mrs Rabbit, smiling. 'Come along in Gingerbread Man. Merry Christmas to you.'

What a feast they had that day! They played games and sang songs until it was almost dark. Then it was time for the gingerbread man to go home. 'Thank you for a lovely day,' he said politely. 'But who was it left me my presents Mrs Rabbit? I didn't see him at all.'

'Why, that was Father Christmas,' she said kindly. 'And not even a gingerbread man can see him.'

The gingerbread man felt very happy as he went wearily home. And he sang a happy, tired song.

'A gingerbread man really loves Christmas
    Day,
With presents and dinners and games to play.
The stars in the sky are as bright as can be,
And dear Father Christmas remembered me!'

And he gave an extra special little skip, just to say, thank you.

7

The Gingerbread Man
and the Stoat

One day the gingerbread man said to himself, 'Brrrrr! It is so cold this morning that I shall need to run and jump a very great deal to make myself warm.' And at once he dashed quickly away over the frosty tussocks of grass, springing over the places where snow still lay. He ran so fast and so far that soon he didn't know where he was. He stopped and scratched his gingerbread head. 'This is a new place where I have never been,' he said.

Suddenly there was a hissing sound! Something moved in the frosty grass.

'Oh dear,' said the gingerbread man, putting his hands behind his back. 'Whatever can that be?' And even though he had sung so bravely, all at once he didn't feel very brave. The grass parted in front of him, and a long, flat head appeared, moving from side to side – a head covered in beautiful white fur. A pair of black beady eyes watched the gingerbread man brightly.

'Hello,' said the gingerbread man nervously, moving a little bit further back.

The creature watched him, his head moving this way and that. 'Hello Gingerbread Man,' he said, and stepped into the open, his long thin body as twisty as a ribbon, all covered in white fur. 'What are you doing is these parts? Travelling are you?'

'I was running and jumping,' said the gingerbread man. 'May I ask your name?' he added politely.

'Me? I'm Stoat,' said the creature, and his beady black eyes looked all around, at the grass, at the trees, at the little dark holes beneath roots and branches.

'I'm very pleased to meet you,' said the gingerbread man.

Then, in a flash the stoat leaped through the air! He whisked past the gingerbread man into a clump of grass. There was the sound of squeaking and something running away very fast indeed, and the stoat came out again, looking cross. 'Not enough snow,' he said. 'I don't show up at all when there's lots of snow, I can always catch my dinner. I'm hungry – I could do with a decent meal.' His flat head moved this way and that, watching.

The gingerbread man felt quite frightened. 'What sort of things do you eat?' he asked.

'Anything I can catch,' replied the stoat and his black eyes gleamed. 'Are you good to eat, Gingerbread Man?'

The gingerbread man knew he was in terrible danger. 'I don't think you'd like to eat me,' he said in a very small voice, and then as the stoat's eyes fixed on him he said quickly, 'What do you do when the snow isn't here, Stoat? How do you catch your dinner then?'

The stoat paused, one foot held in the air. 'I change my coat of course,' he said. 'In winter my fur is white, white as frost and snow. In summer I'm brown, brown as good earth and woodland shadows. That way I don't get seen.'

'But I can see you quite clearly,' said the gingerbread man. 'And it's winter now.'

The stoat hissed again. 'Not enough snow. Watch this!' And away he slid, like a fast flat ribbon over the ground. He stopped on a patch of snow, and all that could be seen of him were his bright black eyes.

'Do you see me now, Gingerbread Man?' he called. 'Do you see me?'

'Not one bit of you,' shouted the gingerbread man. Which wasn't surprising, because he was running away as fast as his gingerbread legs would go! And as he ran he sang this song:

'I'm the gingerbread man and I met a fine
   stoat,
And he's long and he's quick with a very
   white coat.
He hunts in the snow and he hunts in the sun,
But he won't catch Gingerbread – look at him
   run!'

And the gingerbread man dashed away across
the frosty fields and the snowy meadows until he
saw his own haystack once again.

   'What a lot there is in the world,' he said to
himself as he hung up his coat. 'What a good
thing I know so much already.' And he put his
hands behind his head and snuggled down in the
warm hay.

8

The Gingerbread Man
and the Flood

When the gingerbread man woke up the next morning he heard a very strange sound. 'Somebody is dancing on my haystack,' he said to himself and looked out to see who it was. But he quickly pulled his head back in again! 'Oh it's you, rain,' he said, laughing. 'Why are you coming down so hard? Look, the field is full of puddles.' But the raindrops only came down harder.

All morning it rained, and all afternoon. The little gingerbread man couldn't go out at all. 'I think it's very mean of you to rain so much,' he said crossly. 'I mustn't get wet or I shall go soft, and everything is wetter than I have ever seen it.' And the raindrops kept on falling, all through the evening and all through the long wet night.

The next day the gingerbread man woke up very early indeed, when it was still quite dark. He could hear splashing sounds, and every now and then a great big splosh as if something large had fallen into a pond. He peered about him. 'Goodness me!' he said in a shocked voice. 'The puddles have come into my haystack! It is wet everywhere and look, my hay is falling into the water!' Sure enough, the water was all around the haystack, and every now and then a large piece of hay would slide down and go all soggy. 'If you come much closer I shall get wet,' said the gingerbread man to the flood, but all he could hear was the lapping of the water as it grew deeper and deeper.

The gingerbread man realized he would have to do something. Quickly he put on his coat and boots and hat, and stood up and looked out across the field. All he could see was water, gleaming in the dim morning light. 'Where has my field gone?' he said crossly. 'All that rain has filled it up.' He looked down – he had hardly any hay left to stand on at all! 'If I get wet I shall go soft and be all gone,' said the gingerbread man in a frightened voice, clasping his hands together. Then he had an idea. He gave a great big jump, as big as any he had ever done on a fine spring morning, and jumped up the haystack. He clung tight to the hay, and all around pieces of it fell into the water. Then he clambered right to the top of the haystack and came out into the cold, wet morning. 'Thank goodness it has stopped raining at last,' he said, pulling his coat around him.

Everywhere he looked there was water, in the fields and meadows, by the hedge and the trees. The gingerbread man's haystack was getting smaller and smaller, as more and more of it fell into the flood. 'I think I had better sing a song,' he said in a not very brave voice.

'When a gingerbread man finds his haystack
    all wet,
It's as horrid a thing as he has seen yet.
He has a warm coat and his feet are still dry,
But who is to save him? Will Gingerbread try?'

But he didn't see what he could do to stop himself getting wet.

Just then the branch of a tree floated by, bobbing up and down on the water. There wasn't a moment to lose. The gingerbread man sprang from his haystack, his coat flapping out behind him, and landed amongst the bare winter twigs. 'Goodness me,' he said to himself. 'What a lucky gingerbread man I am. My haystack has almost gone to nothing.' And as he watched, the very last of the haystack slid into the water. It made the gingerbread man very sad, even though he had escaped. 'I did so like my haystack,' he said sadly.

The branch bobbed away across the flooded fields, going this way and that, blown by the wind, until it stuck fast in a hedge. The gingerbread man parted the twigs and looked out. There, right in front of him, was Snail, clinging fast to the hedge but still not far from the water.

'What are you doing, Snail?' asked the gingerbread man. 'Why don't you climb higher?'

'I am climbing as fast as I can,' said Snail. 'You know how slow I am.'

'I think you had better join me on my branch,' said the gingerbread man, and carefully helped the snail creep aboard, his house swaying as he moved.

Just then the wind blew and the branch floated away again, across the great sheet of water. The gingerbread man laughed. 'I like floating about on a branch,' he said happily. 'But what shall I do Snail, now that my haystack has gone? Where shall I go to keep myself warm and dry?'

The snail lifted up his strange, spiky head. 'You must find somewhere new, Gingerbread Man. See, it is going to rain again.' And he ducked into the house which he carried on his back.

'What shall I do, what shall I do?' cried the gingerbread man, gazing up at the great black clouds. 'I shall get wet, and there will be nothing left of me!'

But this time the rainclouds heard the little gingerbread man, and big and fierce as they were

they rumbled to one another. 'Let's not rain any more today. We shall spoil the little ginger-bread man!'

The gingerbread man puffed his cheeks out with relief and sang himself a song.

'The snail has a house that is heavy and
    strong,
But a gingerbread man must scamper along!
Now, where can he stay in the warm and the dry,
To wait for the summer to come by and by?'

And he sat down on his branch, bobbing along on the water, and wondered what would happen.

9

The Gingerbread Man
Has a Gallop

All night the gingerbread man and the snail clung to their branch. All night the wind blew and they floated this way and that. When morning came they were quite, quite lost.

'Will it be like this for ever, Snail?' asked the gingerbread man, gazing out at the shining water. 'Won't the ground ever come back?'

The snail grunted and waved his horns. 'Don't be in such a hurry. See, already the water is going.'

True enough, here and there the grass was poking through once again, and soon they passed a hedge where there was a lot of dry ground. The snail stretched his head out, waggling his horns so that he could see. 'This is a fine place for a snail,' he said. 'I should like to stay here.' So the gingerbread man caught hold of a grassy tussock and pulled the branch to shore. Then the snail crept on to the ground.

'Thank you, Gingerbread,' he said slowly, waving his horns. 'There is no room in my house or I would ask you to share it.'

'Oh, I'm sure I shall be all right,' said the gingerbread man bravely. 'A gingerbread man is good at adventures!' And at once he pushed the branch back on to the water, and stood waving until the snail was out of sight.

There was still a great deal of water about and the gingerbread man wondered how long it would be before he too could leave the branch. 'If I wasn't so brave I should be frightened,' he said to himself, settling his conker hat a little more firmly on his head.

Suddenly there was an enormous crashing and splashing, louder than anything the ginger-bread man had ever heard. 'If I wasn't made of gingerbread I should be very frightened indeed,' he told himself, and clung tight to his branch with his gingerbread hands. The crashing and splashing grew louder still. A horse burst from beyond some trees and came galloping through the water towards the little gingerbread man, neighing and throwing his head about in fright.

'What shall I do, what shall I do?' screamed the horse.

'If you don't stop splashing you will make me wet,' cried the gingerbread man.

'What do I care for that,' neighed the horse. 'I am lost, my field is gone.'

'How very silly you are,' said the gingerbread

man. 'The water will be gone soon and then you will have green grass to eat.'

'What do I care for that?' said the horse. 'My stable is warm and dry, full of good things, and I shall never see it again.'

'Then you are even more silly,' said the gingerbread man crossly. 'Your stable will still be there. Now, if you were a gingerbread man and your haystack had quite, quite gone, that would be different.' He thought for a minute then had an idea. 'Horse, lie down and I shall jump up on your back and ride you to your stable.'

The horse stopped splashing and stared at him. 'Oh please, Gingerbread Man,' he said. 'Please take me home.'

So the horse lay down and the gingerbread man gave a great big jump and landed on his back.

He felt a bit scared as the horse stood, and he saw what a long way he was from the ground. Then, far away across the watery fields, he saw the farm. 'This way Horse,' he cried, holding tight to the mane. 'You'll soon be home!'

And away they went, racing through the fields, jumping over the hedges, the little gingerbread man laughing and shouting with excitement. On and on they ran, faster and faster, until the gingerbread man thought he was flying.

Then the horse stopped. 'There is my stable,'

he said happily, and trotted through the mud towards a shed where the door stood open.

'Stop!' cried the gingerbread man. 'I mustn't go there! I ran away from a little old woman and a little old man, and I don't want to be eaten!'

'You'll be safe in my stable,' said the horse, blinking his big eyes. 'You can hide in my straw when the farmer comes.'

The little gingerbread man wasn't at all sure that he should go into the stable. But the horse carried him carefully through the farmyard and into the shed. The straw looked so warm and dry and comfortable after all the water, and the gingerbread man slid down from the horse's back feeling very tired indeed.

'I shan't stay long,' said the gingerbread man, yawning. He sang a sleepy little song.

'The gingerbread man found a horse in a
    flood,
And brought him safe home like Gingerbread
    should.
This stable is warm and full of nice straw,
So I'll sleep here till morning, curled up on
    the floor.'

Which is just what he did.

10

The Gingerbread Man
Gets Broken

The horse's stable was so warm and comfortable, and the gingerbread man was so cold and tired that it was late in the day before he woke up. He stretched and yawned and rustled in the straw. Then he heard a voice. 'What's that moving about over there, Bugle my lad? You got mice in your stable?'

The gingerbread man kept as still as if he had turned into ice. Footsteps came nearer, and nearer. A hand reached down to move aside the straw. 'Horse, Horse, help me!' cried the gingerbread man very loudly.

At once the horse neighed and kicked up his feet, sending the straw in showers all about.

'Whoa there Bugle, whoa there! It's only a mouse!' called the man, but Bugle kept on neighing and kicking.

The little gingerbread man didn't waste a moment. He picked up his conker hat and ran as fast as he had ever run in his life, his coat whirling out behind him. He heard somebody running quickly after him, but the gingerbread man ran so fast that they couldn't catch him.

'Bless me,' said the man. 'I wonder what that can have been in Bugle's stable?' And he went back to see to the horse.

His narrow escape had given the gingerbread man a dreadful fright. He hardly looked where he was going at all, but dashed as fast as he could right into the cow byre. But he ran so quickly that one of the large, sleepy cows became frightened. She jumped up from her warm straw bed and stepped on the little gingerbread man. Snap! The gingerbread man's leg broke quite in two.

'Oh, oh, oh!' cried the gingerbread man, falling down in the straw. 'What shall I do? This bad cow has broken me!'

The cow lowered her great heavy head and looked at him out of her big brown eyes. 'I'm so sorry little man,' she mooed. 'You startled me. I didn't know it was you.'

'What shall I do, what shall I do?' cried the gingerbread man, trying to fix his leg back on. None of his crumbs were missing so the piece fitted exactly, but he was so dry and crisp from his night in the straw that he wouldn't stick together. The gingerbread man began to sob. 'It is the end of me. I shall have to stay here until I am eaten. Bad cow, foolish cow. Oh, oh, oh!'

The cow was so upset by what she had done that she began to moo miserably. 'Poor little Gingerbread Man!' she mooed and all her friends joined in. 'Poor little man! How terrible to be broken!'

The farm cat came into the byre to see what all the fuss was about. She was large and stealthy, with big soft paws. Sometimes she slept in the warm straw of the stable or the byre, and sometimes she curled up on the farmer's chair by the stove in the house. 'What is the matter?' she mewed. 'Why is Dandelion upset?'

'She has broken a little gingerbread man,' mooed all the cows, and the cat went at once to where the little gingerbread man sat crying.

When he looked up and saw the cat he cried out, 'I know you will eat me! The bad cow has broken me and a gingerbread man must be eaten if he can't run or jump. What a sad gingerbread man I am!'

The cat put out her large, soft paw and stroked him. 'I have never seen a gingerbread man before,' she mewed. 'But I shan't eat you. The farmer and his wife feed me every evening, and every morning I have a bowl of cream. I shall look after you, just like a kitten.' And with that, she curled herself around the gingerbread man, her long fur tickling his nose.

The gingerbread man pulled himself a little

upright. His hat had been knocked over one eye and the cat's fur was making him want to sneeze. 'That's all very well,' he said breathlessly. 'But I'm not a kitten, I'm a gingerbread man! I am supposed to run and jump and have adventures.'

The cat stopped purring. 'Don't you like being a kitten?' she asked crossly.

'I like best to be a gingerbread man,' said the gingerbread man politely. 'But now I have a broken leg and soon I shan't be anything. And I was so brave and handsome!' He wanted to cry again, but he tried very hard not to.

The cat uncurled herself. 'What a pity,' she mewed. 'I should have liked to have a kitten. Well, I see I must mend you.'

Without another word she ran from the cow byre. The gingerbread man was left alone with the cows, who mooed kindly and tried to cheer him up. 'I don't think she can mend me,' said the gingerbread man sadly.

'I'm sure she'll try,' said Dandelion in her deep voice.

And in a moment the cat returned, running as quickly as she could. In her mouth was a spoon! And on the spoon was cake mixture! 'The farmer's wife is baking a cake,' she mewed. 'I have stolen her spoon and soon she will come looking for it. Quickly little gingerbread man.'

The gingerbread man picked up his broken leg, that was so dry and crisp, and dipped it in the cake mixture. This time when he fitted it back on it stuck fast! 'I'm mended, I'm mended,' he cried joyfully, and tried to give a very big skip. But the cat stopped him.

'You must be careful, Gingerbread Man,' she said, holding him with her soft paw. 'Your leg isn't dry yet. You must stay safe on the farm until it has grown strong again.'

'But the farm isn't safe. It's where I got broken,' said the gingerbread man. All the same, he knew the cat was right. With only the littlest skip, he went carefully to sit out of Dandelion's way, and he sang a little song.

'When a gingerbread man comes to stay at a
    farm
He has to be careful to keep safe from harm.
When a cow stepped so quickly he was in a fix,
Till mother cat saved him with lovely cake mix!'

'I had better find somewhere safe until I am
well,' he said to himself. 'I wonder where that
might be?' And he put his chin in his gingerbread hands and swung his two gingerbread legs
while he thought.

11

The Gingerbread Man
and the Hens

The little gingerbread man thought and thought, but he couldn't think of anywhere that would be safe for him to stay until his leg was crisp and strong once again. He knew that the cow byre wasn't safe because the cow had stepped on him, and the horse's stable was dangerous because the man came there. 'I must see what there is on this farm,' he said to himself, and running and jumping very gently, he went out into the windy day.

Straw and dust were blowing everywhere, and the gingerbread man had to hold tight to his hat. 'What a horrid day,' he said, and a voice clucked, 'Yes indeed! This wind is ruffling my feathers.'

The little gingerbread man looked to see who had spoken. There was a large brown hen, trying to peck in the ground. Every time she put her head down the wind blew all her feathers the wrong way, and every time she put her head up the wind blew them back again.

'The wind is playing a game,' said the gingerbread man, laughing and clapping his hands.

The hen shook herself. 'I don't like such games,' she said. 'I shall go back to my nice warm henhouse and lay an egg.' She began to run off, her long toes stretching out.

But the gingerbread man called out, 'Wait Hen, please! Is it a nice house? Could I stay in it until my leg is better?'

The hen turned to look over her shoulder. 'We have nice straw in our boxes. Yes, you can come.'

So the gingerbread man went with the hen to her nice warm henhouse, where all the hens sat in the straw to lay their eggs. He sat in the straw too, and was very comfortable. He sang this song.

'The henhouse seems just the right place to be,
When the cold wind is blowing all over me.
I'll stay here until I've grown crisp and strong,
And then I shall dash and hurry along!'

The wind blew harder and harder, and soon it started to rain. The gingerbread man looked out and thought how sensible he was to have found the henhouse.

Just as he was thinking that a large, fat black hen hopped up beside him. 'You are in my place,' she said crossly.

The gingerbread man looked at her. She had very black eyes and a very sharp beak. 'I am sorry,' he said politely. 'I only came in out of the wind, and because I have hurt my leg.'

'You can't stay in my box,' said the hen, and fluttered her feathers at him.

The gingerbread man climbed carefully down and looked for somewhere else to sit. But all the hens had come in out of the wind and rain, and the henhouse was quite full up. 'There isn't anywhere for me,' he said. 'You said I could come here Hen! Where shall I go?'

The brown hen who had asked him in leaned down and called, 'I have laid my egg now, Gingerbread Man. You can come and sit by me.'

So up went the little gingerbread man to sit beside the big brown hen. There wasn't very much room and he had to take care not to be pushed off. All the hens talked about him. 'Isn't he strange?' they said. 'Where are his feathers? He isn't even as pretty as an egg!'

The gingerbread man felt upset. He had always thought he was handsome. 'I have a lovely new coat, and a very nice hat.' he said to himself. 'And my daisy buttons are only a little faded.'

Then the henhouse door opened, and the gingerbread man heard the sound of footsteps! 'It's the farmer come to get the eggs,' said all the hens to each other.

The gingerbread man clasped his hands together. 'What shall I do, what shall I do?' he asked the brown hen. 'I shall be caught!'

'Hide under my feathers,' clucked the hen. And without thinking, the gingerbread man crept underneath her. Right next to him was a big, brown, egg!

He stayed very, very still. 'Now then Brownie,' said a voice, and a great big hand reached under the hen and felt around for the egg. The little gingerbread man was so frightened he thought he would shake into crumbs! But, bravely, he put his two gingerbread hands against the egg and pushed it towards the farmer's fingers. The egg was lifted out. 'That's the way,' said the farmer. 'You're turning into a right good hen, Brownie.' And he took the basket of eggs and went out of the shed.

The little gingerbread man climbed down. 'I don't think that's a safe place to be,' he said, shaking the straw from his coat. 'Perhaps I had better sit on the floor.' And down he sat, on the hard earth, and tried to rest.

Soon it was night-time, and all the hens went to sleep, clucking quietly to themselves. Then there was a strange scratching on the wooden wall. The gingerbread man sat up. 'What can that be?' he said to himself. The scratching came again. 'Oh dear,' said the gingerbread man.

'Something is making a hole in the wall. Something wants to get in!' The hens clucked and moved a little closer to each other. The hole got bigger and bigger. 'Doesn't anyone know what it is?' asked the gingerbread man, but the hens just clucked a little more. The gingerbread man felt almost as frightened as he had when the farmer came. But, bravely, he went to look out of the hole. And there, right outside, scrabbling to get in, was Red Fox!

'I see him, I see him,' she said hungrily. 'I shall have a tasty fat hen and a tasty little gingerbread man for my dinner. I see him!'

'It is Red Fox!' cried the gingerbread man. 'Quickly hens, we must stop her!' But the hens just clucked and rustled their feathers.

The gingerbread man saw that he must stop Red Fox by himself. At once he began to pick up all the pieces of straw that had fallen from the nest boxes, and push them into the hole. Each time Red Fox tried to bite or scrabble her way in, the straw got in the way. 'Stop it Gingerbread Man!' she said crossly. 'It's nearly morning and soon I must go. I want a tasty hen for my dinner!'

'Go away Red Fox,' said the gingerbread man. 'I shan't let you in!' And at last the fox did go away, swishing her fine red tail angrily.

The gingerbread man sat down to rest. He was very tired. 'Thank you Gingerbread Man,' clucked the hens. 'We were so frightened of Red Fox that we didn't know what to do. Come and sit with us, won't you?'

But the gingerbread man shook his head. 'A henhouse is no place for a gingerbread man,' he said. And because he was so tired he sang a rather sad song.

'The hens in the henhouse don't seem to be
As kind as Gingerbread hoped they would be.
There isn't much room and Red Fox came
    along,
So I won't stay here to get crisp and strong!'

'I think I had better find somewhere else,' he said sadly.

12

The Gingerbread Man
Has a Fright

The gingerbread man went out of the henhouse as soon as it was light. The wind was still blowing quite hard, and the ground was wet with puddles. He pulled his coat close round him. 'If only the sun would shine I would soon be crisp and strong again,' he said crossly. 'Sun, Sun, shine for me!' But the sun in winter is a very long way away from the world, and although it shone as hard as it could, it didn't make the ginger-bread man better.

The little gingerbread man was tired of winter. 'How silly the sun is,' he said. 'I see I must find somewhere warm and dry. But with cows and hens all around there isn't anywhere for me.' And he put his hands on his hips and looked about him.

Just then the cat came out of the hay barn. 'Hello,' called the gingerbread man. 'Is that a warm place for me?'

The cat walked on soft paws towards him. 'It is certainly very warm,' she said, licking her fur with her pink tongue. 'It's full of hay, you see.'

'Then it will suit me very well,' said the ginger-bread man. 'I had a haystack once and that was very nice.'

The cat stopped licking her fur and licked the gingerbread man instead. 'I do wish you were a kitten,' she purred. 'I should so like to lick you.'

'A gingerbread man doesn't like being licked,' said the gingerbread man firmly, and marched quickly off to the hay barn.

The barn was full of lovely soft hay. The gingerbread man lay down in it and kicked his legs happily. 'I *am* feeling better,' he said. 'Soon I shall be quite well again. How nice it is to have a warm hay bed once more.' He felt so pleased that he sang a song.

'On a wild, wet, windy winter's day,
Gingerbread can't find many games to play.
But the hay barn is just the right sort of place
Where a gingerbread man can run and chase.'

At that he jumped up and down in the hay, which was so soft that it didn't hurt his leg at all. He gave an extra big jump, and the hay covered him up and tickled his nose. 'This is fun,' he said to himself. 'But I do wish I had someone to play with.'

'Crick, crick,' said a voice. 'I will play with you, Gingerbread Man!' The gingerbread man looked round. There was a creature very like a mouse, but much bigger. It had a long, pink tail. 'Who are you?' he asked, feeling a little frightened.

The creature smiled and showed rows of sharp teeth. 'I am Rat,' it said. 'And I live in the hay barn. Let's chase each other!'

The gingerbread man wasn't sure that he wanted to be chased by the rat, so he said, 'I will chase you first.' The rat smiled slyly and said, 'Crick, crick,' once again.

Off they went. The rat ran swiftly up and down the hay, through the piles and the hummocks, this way and that with the gingerbread man chasing him. Then he called, 'I shall chase *you* now, Gingerbread!'

But the gingerbread man called back, 'Oh no! I must catch you first!'

So they ran and chased again, the rat going up and down, this way and that, through the piles and hummocks until he called again, 'It is time to change! It is my turn to chase!'

But again the gingerbread man called out, 'I haven't caught you yet! We must keep on running.'

The gingerbread man was getting very tired, but he dared not stop chasing the rat. At last the rat stopped, and lay down panting. 'I cannot run any more,' he said wearily.

'I am not tired at all,' said the gingerbread man, although he too was quite out of breath, and sat in the hay, swinging his legs.

Suddenly the barn door swung wide open – in rushed the wind, tossing the hay this way and that. 'The farmer is coming!' squeaked the rat. 'Crick, crick!' And in a flash he was gone, running to hide in his hole.

'What shall I do, what shall I do?' moaned the gingerbread man, wringing his gingerbread hands. 'Where can I hide?' He looked all around, but there was nothing but hay.

'This is a windy day,' said a great big voice. The gingerbread man was so frightened that he gave a great big jump and landed right in the middle of a great pile of hay. He lay very, very still.

Swish, swish! The gingerbread man peeped out to see what was happening. The farmer was scooping the hay up on a fork and putting it into a cart. Suddenly he felt himself flying through the air! The farmer had scooped up the pile of hay the gingerbread man was in and put it in the cart.

'Whatever shall I do?' whispered the gingerbread man to himself. 'Where can I be going?'

More and more hay was put on the cart and the gingerbread man became more and more worried. At last the farmer stopped scooping hay and began pulling the cart. 'This is a very strange thing to happen to a gingerbread man,' said the gingerbread man to himself. 'What a good thing it is that I am brave and clever, or I should be very frightened.'

The cart didn't go very far. As soon as it stopped the farmer began scooping again. All at once the gingerbread man found himself whizzing through the air even faster than before, to land with a flump upside down in his pile of hay. He was so cross he forgot to be frightened. 'I don't like being scooped!' he said loudly, struggling to his feet. 'What has happened to me? Where have I been scooped to?' And he pushed his way out of the hay.

He stopped in surprise. He was in a hayrack, high off the floor. And there was Dandelion the cow, her big nose and soft brown eyes right in front of him. 'Hello Gingerbread Man,' she mooed. 'Are you better? Why are you in my hay?'

'I was scooped,' said the gingerbread man crossly. 'And I am quite better thank you. Stand still while I jump on your nose Dandelion. I must get down from here.' With that he jumped on to Dandelion's nose, ran between her horns, across her back and down her tail just as if it was a rope. But this time he didn't go near her great big feet!

'It's time I left this farm,' he said, settling his conker hat on his head.

'Goodbye Gingerbread Man,' mooed Dandelion.

The cat by the gate mewed, 'Goodbye.'

And the hens in the yard clucked 'Goodbye,' too.

'A farmyard's no place for a gingerbread man,' said the gingerbread man, and he began to run and jump, back to the fields and the meadows. 'Look how crisp and strong I am!' he shouted, and he jumped on a tussock of grass and turned a cartwheel, because he was just as good as he had ever been!

13

The Gingerbread Man Alone

The gingerbread man was so pleased to be back in the fields once again that he ran and jumped for a very long time. Then he bounced from a tussock of grass to a hummock of earth and sang this song:

'A gingerbread man should always be
Running about in the fine country.
He won't catch cold and he won't be sad,
For Gingerbread knows he should always be
   glad!'

He put his hands on his hips and looked about him. The sky was very clear and cold, and there was no sound anywhere. 'Where is everyone?' he said to himself. 'I must run and jump some more and find where everybody has gone on this cold winter's day.' And off went the little gingerbread man once again, running and jumping to see what he could see.

After a while he was tired, and sat down beneath a hedge to rest. 'I don't know where everyone has gone,' he said crossly. 'There is no one at all to talk to.'

'Chirrup. Chirrup,' said a voice. 'Hello, Gingerbread Man.'

The little gingerbread man looked up. There, sitting fluffed up in the hedge, was a sparrow.

'Why are you sitting there Sparrow, and not flying about?' asked the gingerbread man.

'Because it is such a cold day,' said the little sparrow, fluffing up his feathers even more. 'In winter I have to keep warm. Sometimes I wish I had flown away, like the swallows, until the summer. It is so cold today that I shall just sit here quietly. Do you want to sit next to me Gingerbread?'

'Oh no,' said the gingerbread man, laughing. 'A gingerbread man must run and jump all the time. I don't mind the cold.' And with that, he turned a cartwheel and raced off across the fields once again.

Just then a few flakes of snow began to fall. 'I see I must find shelter,' said the gingerbread man, and raced quickly to a large oak tree. The tree's wide branches kept out all the snow. The little gingerbread man sat down on a large pebble. 'I shall be very comfortable now,' he said happily.

Then the pebble began to move! 'What is

happening?' said the little gingerbread man, grabbing at his hat to stop it falling off. 'What are you doing Pebble? You're not supposed to move.'

'Silly little gingerbread man,' said a voice. 'I'm not a pebble!' And out popped the snail's spiky head.

The gingerbread man clapped his gingerbread hands when he saw his friend. 'I didn't mean to sit on you, Snail,' he said. 'Won't you stay and talk to me?'

'I can't stay long,' said the snail, waving his horns. 'Brrrr! It's too cold to be out on a day like this. What you need is a house, Gingerbread.'

'I'd rather have someone to talk to,' said the gingerbread man. 'I want to talk about the frost and the pretty snow, and the wind chasing the leaves, and the great grey clouds that bump about the sky. I want to talk about winter.'

The snail sniffed. 'Winter's nothing for a snail to talk about,' he said. 'Not when he's got a nice warm house. Goodbye, Gingerbread!' And the snail disappeared back into his shell.

The little gingerbread man was tired of being by himself. As soon as the snow stopped he ran off through the fields, leaving little holes in the snow where his feet had been. Soon he came to the beehive. 'Perhaps the bees will talk to me,' he said. He knocked on the door and called, 'Who is there? Won't someone talk to me?'

But all he heard was a sleepy buzzing and a voice which said, 'Go away, whoever you are. We won't wake up till spring.'

'Goodness me, everyone's asleep,' said the gingerbread man. He began to walk along the bottom of the hedge, where the leaves were thick and dry, and he kicked them up as he went along. 'Ouch!' he cried suddenly. 'My foot has been prickled! Who has prickled me?' And there was the hedgehog, curled up in a tight, prickly ball. 'Wake up Hedgehog! Hedgehog wake up!' called the gingerbread man, trying to shake the prickly ball without hurting his hands. But the hedgehog stayed curled up as tight as anything, and all the gingerbread man heard was a long, hedgehog snore.

The little gingerbread man felt very sad. 'I haven't anyone to talk to,' he said, and trudged along beside the hedge.

'Caaark! Caaark!' The gingerbread man knew that sound!

'I don't want to talk you *you*, Crow!' he shouted and began to dash away as fast as he could.

'I wants a piece of gingerbread, I does!' croaked the crow. 'A body can't get a decent feed in winter. Now's my chance, now I shall get him!'

'Oh no you won't,' cried the gingerbread man, and he raced away.

The little gingerbread man ran very fast indeed. But the crow's dirty wings flapped faster still, faster and faster, nearer and nearer. Snap! The crow's yellow claws snapped shut. 'Got you!' he cried. 'Caaark! Caaark!'

'Silly old crow,' shouted the gingerbread man rudely. 'You haven't got me at all.'

The crow flapped his wings and stared at his dirty yellow claws. Instead of the gingerbread man he held tight to a great lump of frosty grass. He shook it to see if it really might be the gingerbread man. 'Where's he gone? Where's he gone?' he muttered. 'I wants a tasty piece of gingerbread, I does.'

And the little gingerbread man, hiding safe under a big piece of brown winter bracken, laughed to himself. 'He won't catch me,' he said, and sang a little song.

'There's one thing a gingerbread man always knows,
When the cold winter wind hurts his gingerbread toes.
When he seems quite alone in the frost and the snow,
There's sure to be someone – a nasty black crow!'

He was still laughing when he went to sleep that night, huddled in his coat under a pile of leaves. 'This may be all right for a hedgehog but it isn't very good for a gingerbread man,' he said, tucking his hands inside his coat to try to warm them. 'Whatever shall I do tomorrow?'

14

The Gingerbread Man
Needs a House

The gingerbread man woke up very stiff and cold from his night in the leaves. 'It's a great pity that my haystack was spoiled,' he said to himself. 'Perhaps a gingerbread man does need a house sometimes.' And stretching himself, he went off to find one.

First he went to the snail, who was still under the oak tree, curled up in his shell. 'Snail! Snail!' called the gingerbread man. 'Tell me where I can find a house.'

The snail came out slowly and grumpily. 'You woke me up,' he said crossly.

'But I need a house,' said the gingerbread man. 'I don't like sleeping in leaves, my ginger-bread goes soggy. Where can I find a house, Snail?'

The snail peered at the gingerbread man with his horns. 'There are lots of houses. Let me see. Do you want a house like mine? It is the best sort of house to my way of thinking, because it is always with you.'

The gingerbread man laughed. 'Oh no,' he

said. 'I couldn't run and jump if I had to carry my house about.'

'Well then,' said the snail. 'Would you like a nest, high up in a tree, safe from Red Fox and her children?'

Again the gingerbread man laughed. 'Oh no,' he said. 'The rain would make me wet and the crow would catch me.'

'Well then,' said the snail. 'You must have a hole in the ground. Would you like that, Gingerbread?'

At this the little gingerbread man clapped his hands. 'Yes, yes!' he cried. 'I can have a hole to live in, like the rabbits. Where can I find a hole, Snail?'

The snail thought for a moment. 'You had better ask Mole,' he said at last.

'Thank you, thank you Snail,' said the gingerbread man, and ran off at once to find the mole.

He hadn't run very far when he came to a big ploughed field. 'Will Mole be here I wonder,' he said to himself. And he called, 'Mole! Mole! Are you digging here?'

But the wind blew across the dark brown earth and no mole appeared. So the gingerbread man ran on until he came to a stream. Again he called out 'Mole, Mole, are you digging here?'

But the stream gurgled over the stones and no

mole appeared. So the gingerbread man ran on until he came to a grassy meadow. 'Mole, Mole, are you digging here?' he called once again. The grass rustled all about him and no mole appeared.

Suddenly up popped a little black head and two wide pink paws, straight out of the ground right in front of the gingerbread man. The little gingerbread man was so surprised that he sat down with a great big flump!

'Goodness me, goodness me,' said the mole, twitching his nose and peering with his little black eyes. 'What is this I see? A gingerbread man?'

The gingerbread man stood up, feeling rather silly. 'Hello Mole,' he said shyly. 'Snail said you would find me a house.'

'House? House?' said the mole, shaking the earth from his whiskers. 'Holes is what I know, just holes. Best house ever a hole is. Want a hole do you?'

'Yes please,' said the gingerbread man. 'A nice dry hole so I won't get wet and the wind won't blow me to crumbs.'

'I see, I see,' said the mole, pulling himself all the way out of the ground. 'Come this way. Come this way.'

So the gingerbread man followed the mole as he bustled across the field, finding the way with

his twitching nose and scrabbling along with his big flat paws. 'You have a very fine coat,' said the gingerbread man politely.

The mole stopped and brushed his velvet black tummy. 'Nice of you to say so. Yes . . . well . . . proud of it meself,' he said, and then bustled off again, twice as quickly.

Soon they came to a small hill. The mole went up a little way and began sniffing and scrabbling in the grass. 'This is the place, this is the place,' he muttered. 'Dry on a hill. Out of the wind. This is the place for a gingerbread man.'

'But there isn't a hole,' said the gingerbread man.

'Soon will be. Soon will be,' said the mole. He scrabbled around a little more. Then down went his head, up went his tail, and all four feet went scrabble, scrabble, scrabble! The earth flew up so quickly that the gingerbread man had to jump out of the way. In no time at all the mole had dug a hole for the gingerbread man.

'There you are. There you are,' he said, dusting off his smooth, black tummy.

The gingerbread man tried to squeeze himself into the hole. 'The door is too small,' he said, huffing and puffing as he tried to get inside.

'Good sense that is. Good sense,' said the mole. 'Don't want things trying to get in.'

'But I can hardly get in!' said the gingerbread

man, squashing himself through. 'Though it is lovely inside,' he added, because the mole had been very kind to dig a hole for him.

'Glad you like it. Glad you like it,' said the mole, and began to bustle off.

'Thank you Mole,' called the gingerbread man. 'Thank you very much.'

The mole turned round, his long nose twitching. 'Just you remember. Just you remember,' he said sternly. 'Keep the door small. Good sense that is.'

'All right' said the gingerbread man, waving.

As soon as the mole had gone the gingerbread man had a good look at his hole. It was very nice inside – warm and dry and snug. But the door was so small that he really could hardly squeeze through it. 'Never mind,' he said to himself. 'I shall be very comfortable here.' And he sang himself a little song.

'The wind may blow and the rain may fall,
But Gingerbread just doesn't care at all.
He's cosy and warm like a very small mouse,
A gingerbread man in a very small house!

And because he hadn't slept very well in the leaves, he gave a great big yawn and fell fast asleep.

15

The Gingerbread Man
in Danger

The gingerbread man slept very well in the hole the mole had dug for him, and in the morning he yawned and stretched and thought how lucky he was. 'I shall go out and run and jump and play, and when I am tired, or it is raining, I shall come back to my hole and wait for spring,' he said to himself. Out he went, squeezing himself through the door, and off into the bright cold day. The sun was shining on the puddles, and the little gingerbread man danced and jumped over them, because he could see himself in the water. 'What a handsome gingerbread man I am,' he shouted happily.

He ran to the edge of a little wood on top of a hill. The trees waved their bare branches as the wind went shoosh, shoosh in them.

'Hello Gingerbread Man.' A squirrel ran headfirst down a tree to talk to him.

'Hello Squirrel,' said the gingerbread man. 'Isn't it a lovely day?'

'Yes indeed,' said the squirrel. 'I woke up and found I was hungry, and as it was such a nice day

I came out to get my nuts. I've got lots. Would you like some?'

'Yes please,' said the gingerbread man eagerly. He stretched out his gingerbread hands and the squirrel put the nuts into them, the shells already cracked by the squirrel's sharp teeth.

The gingerbread man and the squirrel sat side by side and ate lots and lots of nuts. Soon the gingerbread man couldn't eat any more. 'I'm full up,' he said in a fat sort of voice. 'I can't eat one more nut.'

The squirrel yawned. 'I shall go back to bed. Not long to spring, I don't suppose. Goodbye, Gingerbread.'

'Goodbye,' said the gingerbread man, standing up. 'I think I had better go back to my house. I have a hole you know. A very nice hole.'

But the squirrel wasn't listening. He was running straight up to a tree and along the branches, swinging and running and jumping back to his nest. So the gingerbread man tried to run too, but he was so full of nuts he could only just skip. By the time he reached his hole he was very sleepy. 'I shall squeeze in here and lie down until I feel better' he said to himself.

So he squeezed and squeezed and squeezed. His hat fell off, plop! But he didn't get into the hole. 'Oh dear me,' he puffed, sitting down for a rest. 'I told the mole he had made the door too small.' So he took off his coat and tried again. He squeezed and squeezed and squeezed. But still he couldn't get in. 'Whatever shall I do?' he said, looking at his big fat tummy. 'I should like to lie down in my nice warm hole.'

Just then a rabbit hopped by. 'Why are you looking sad, Gingerbread Man?' she asked. 'What's the matter?'

'I can't get into my hole,' said the gingerbread man.

The rabbit looked at the fat little gingerbread man and the thin little hole. She put her paw up to her mouth and laughed. 'You've eaten too much! You'll have to dig a bigger hole, Gingerbread Man!'

'What a good idea,' said the gingerbread man, clapping his hands. And at once he picked up a large flat stone and began making the hole bigger.

'Be careful Gingerbread,' called the rabbit, hopping away. 'Don't make it too big – that would be dangerous.'

'I won't,' called the gingerbread man, digging as hard as he could.

The little gingerbread man dug and dug and dug. Soon he could get into the hole quite easily. But he didn't stop! 'This is a much nicer hole,' he said to himself, 'with a much nicer door. I shall take lots of nice things into my hole. I shall have

this stone, and these thistles, and a nice bunch of twigs to sweep the floor. What a fine hole it will be!' And on and on he dug, making the hole bigger and bigger, and putting more and more things inside.

At last the little gingerbread man felt tired. 'I have made a beautiful hole,' he said happily. 'And I shall go inside and have a long, long sleep.' Into the hole went the gingerbread man and settled down on a pile of dried brown leaves. Soon he was fast asleep.

Night came. The moon shone her silver light over the fields and the meadows. The owls hooted in the far forest, the stoat started on his stealthy way, and Red Fox sniffed the night air and said to herself, 'This is a fine bright night for hunting.' The little gingerbread man slept in his fine, big hole and dreamed happy dreams.

Red Fox paused as she trotted through the meadow to the farmyard. 'What is this I see?' she said softly. 'What a fine big hole has been dug here. There must be a fine tasty morsel inside a hole such as this. How pleased my children will be when I catch it for them!'

Slowly, slowly, so very slowly, Red Fox crept up to the hole. Her long red nose pointed out in front, and her long red tail stretched out behind. She licked her lips and her white teeth gleamed in the moonlight.

Just then the little gingerbread man woke up. He stretched and yawned, and looked about his fine big hole. The moonlight was shining through the door and making his lovely things look all silver. 'What a good thing I am such a clever gingerbread man,' he said happily. There was a faint rustling in the grass outside the hole. 'I wonder what this is,' he said, getting up. He put his head out of the hold – and there was Red Fox!

'Oh, oh, oh!' cried the little gingerbread man.

'Gingerbread! By my red fur, Gingerbread,' hissed Red Fox. And she pushed her long red paw right into the hole, reaching out to grab the little gingerbread man.

Bravely, the little gingerbread man seized one of the thistles in his gingerbread hands. Without a moment's thought he rushed at Red Fox and struck her hard on her nose with the thistle. Bang bang went the little gingerbread man with his thistle. 'Ow! Ow!' cried Red Fox, as the thistle hurt her. 'Stop it Gingerbread Man, stop it! I shall come into your hole.'

'Oh no you won't,' cried the gingerbread man, and hit her again. It was too much for Red Fox. She turned and ran, taking her sore nose away into the woods and the fields.

The little gingerbread man sat down, panting.

His gingerbread legs were shaking so much he thought he might turn into crumbs. 'The mole was right,' he said sadly. 'I should not have made my hole so big.' And he sang a little song.

'When a gingerbread man goes to live in a hole
That is dug for him by a very kind mole,
He must be sure to do as he's told,
Or Red Fox will come in, out of the cold!'

The little gingerbread man didn't sleep any more that night. He stayed awake, holding tight to his thistle, wondering what was to come.

The Gingerbread Man
and the Spring

The little gingerbread man felt very tired after his night staying awake in case Red Fox came to catch him. He knew that he had been silly not to listen to the mole and the rabbit. 'I'm not as clever as I thought,' he said sadly, and put on his coat and hat and boots to go out and see what sort of day it was.

He was so tired and sad that he didn't jump or skip at all, but plodded along looking down at the ground. He didn't see how brightly the sun was shining. Soon he came to a stream, rushing and bubbling over the stones. The gingerbread man felt rather hot. 'I shall sit here and rest,' he said, and settled down on a rock. But the sun kept on shining, and the gingerbread man felt so hot that he unfastened his coat. He could see himself in the stream's bright water. 'What a pity my daisy buttons are so faded,' he said sadly. 'I'm not nearly as handsome as I used to be.' And up he got to go on his way.

Just then a blackbird began singing in the hedge, opening his beak wide and whistling as hard as he could. 'Why don't you sing with me, Gingerbread?' he called. 'We should all sing today!'

'I don't feel like singing,' said the gingerbread man, and he walked on.

Mrs Rabbit popped out of her hole. 'Hello Gingerbread!' she called. 'You're all muffled up on this fine sunny morning!'

'Hello Mrs Rabbit,' said the gingerbread man dismally. 'I have to keep warm, you see.'

'Warm! You look more than warm, you look hot little Gingerbread Man. But I must get on, I've my spring cleaning to do.' And she shook her duster and rushed back to her hole.

The little gingerbread man's currant eyes nearly popped out of his head. 'Is it spring?' he said to himself. 'Is it the end of winter?' He began to hurry along as fast as he could, looking for someone who would tell him if spring had come at last. But his coat was so hot that soon he had to sit down in the shade of a hedge to rest. A tiny primrose nodded shyly up at him. 'Is it spring little flower?' asked the gingerbread man. The primrose said nothing at all, but she nodded, shyly.

The gingerbread man took off his coat and put it over his arm. Then he got up and hurried on his way. 'Grunt, grunt.' There, bustling across the meadow, was the hedgehog. 'Have you finished sleeping, Hedgehog?' called the ginger-bread man. 'Is it spring?'

'Silly questions you ask,' said the hedgehog rudely. He went on his way, his long nose poking at the fresh green shoots that rose above the tired, winter grass.

Now the gingerbread man felt so hot that he took off his hat and carried it. He saw the crow flying quickly from tree to tree, carrying twigs and grass in his beak. The gingerbread man was so worried about spring that he forgot to be frightened. He called, 'Crow, please talk to me. Is this spring?'

The crow glared at the gingerbread man out of his yellow eye. 'As if I've time to chatter! A body's got a nest to see to. Can't stop to talk. Caark, Caark!' And he flapped on his way.

By this time the little gingerbread man was so hot that he sat down and took off his nice warm boots. 'All these things are very heavy,' he said to himself. 'How I wish it could be spring!'

A bee came and settled right on his nose! 'Buzzz! Hello Gingerbread Man! You do look hot.' She flew on to his tummy and tickled him.

The little gingerbread man laughed. 'Hello Bee. I should like to run and jump and chase but my coat is too heavy. Is it spring do you think?'

'Buzzz! Of course it is!' said the bee, whizzing round the gingerbread man so fast it made him

dizzy. 'Can't you see how the sun is shining? Can't you hear the birds singing? And the trees are growing new leaves once again, and all the flowers are waiting for me! Don't you just feel so, so happy?' And the bee buzzed up and down in delight.

The little gingerbread man clapped his hands. 'No more snow?' he said. 'No more frost? No more fierce wind or horrid rain?'

'Just gentle showers and breezes,' buzzed the bee happily. 'It is spring. Spring! Spring!' And away she flew to the meadows and the gardens where the flowers bloomed once again.

The little gingerbread man jumped and

jumped for joy. He looked up at the blue sky and the yellow sun high above and he called, 'Thank you Sun! Thank you for spring!' Then he picked up his coat and hat and boots and hurried across the new green grass, saying, 'Thank you Grass! Thank you for spring!' And then because everything looked so fresh and new, he threw wide his gingerbread arms and cried, 'Thank you World! Thank you, thank you for spring!'

Soon he came to Mrs Rabbit's house. 'Mrs Rabbit! Mrs Rabbit!' he called.

Out popped Mrs Rabbit. 'Oh, it's you again!' she beamed, dusting her paws on her apron. 'Still with that heavy coat I see, and on a day like this.'

The gingerbread man held out his clothes. 'Can you keep them for me, kind Mrs Rabbit?' he asked. 'It is spring, and a gingerbread man must run and jump and play!'

Mrs Rabbit took the coat and hat and boots. 'You'll not be needing these for a while,' she said. 'Off with you now and have fun. That's what a gingerbread man's meant for, after all.'

The little gingerbread man dashed on his way. He felt so light and free and happy he almost thought he could fly. The warm spring breeze fluttered three little daisies in the grass. The gingerbread man stopped and said happily. 'Oh! How lucky I am! Now I can have new daisy

buttons.' And he popped them on to his gingerbread front. Then he sang his best, springtime
song.

'I'm a gingerbread man, so handsome and
    strong.
The sun shines bright as I hurry along.
I've seen the dark winter, but now it is spring,
And Gingerbread's happy as anything!'

'What adventures will I have now?' he wondered
as he turned cartwheels across the meadow.
'Such a fine, handsome, springtime gingerbread
man as I am is sure to have fun!' And do you
know – he was right!

Gingerbread Man Recipe

Makes 18–20 gingerbread men

You will need:

200 g plain flour
75 g soft brown sugar
75 g butter
2 tablespoons golden syrup
1 level teaspoon baking powder
2 level teaspoons ground ginger
½ level teaspoon bicarbonate of soda

Method

1. Sift the flour, baking powder, ginger and bicarbonate of soda into a large mixing bowl.

2. Melt the butter, sugar and syrup in a saucepan over a low heat. Do not allow the mixture to get hot.

3. Pour the melted mixture into the mixing

bowl and stir into the dry ingredients with a wooden spoon, until you have a dough.

4. When the dough has cooled a little, turn it out on to a floured board and knead for a few minutes. Then roll the dough out to a thickness of about ½ cm. With a gingerbread man cutter, stamp out as many gingerbread men as you can.

5. You can then give your gingerbread men eyes and buttons using the currants.

6. Bake in a preheated oven at 200°C or Gas Mark 6 for about 10–15 minutes, or until the gingerbread men are slightly brown around the edges.

7. Allow the gingerbread men to cool for about five minutes before lifting them off carefully, and placing on a wire rack. When they are completely cold and firm, store in an airtight tin.